My LITTLE PONY

ANNUAL 2013

Editor: Amanda Clifford
Deputy Editor: Julie Patten
Art Editor: Karen Boller

Licensed By:

Licensed by HASBRO and its logo, MY LITTLE PONY and all related characers are trademarks of Hasbro and are used with permission.
© 2012 Hasbro. All rights reserved

ISBN 978-0-9556380-2-2

Signature Publishing Limited
the last word in publishing

FRIENDSHIP is MAGIC
see more at:
www.MYLiTTLEPONY.com

Watch My Little Pony on TV!
hub
Hubworld.com

HUB is a trademark of Hub Television Networks, LLC and is used with permission.

Published by
Signature Publishing Limited,
Headley House, Headley Road,
Grayshott, Surrey, GU26 6TU
www.signaturepl.co.uk

This belongs to

Age:

WHAT'S INSIDE!

MEET THE PONIES

Here is Princess Celestia and her pony Subjects!

PRINCESS CELESTIA

The wise and beautiful ruler of Equestria has both a unicorn's horn and pegasus' wings. Princess Celestia is supremely magical and all the ponies in Ponyville look up to her and listen to her advice.

TWILIGHT SPARKLE

She's clever, talented and a natural born leader. Twilight Sparkle loves to spend time with her Ponyville pals and use her special skills to share the magic of friendship.

APPLEJACK

Applejack is Ponyville's resident farm gal! She lives with her family at Sweet Apple Acres and is never afraid of getting her hooves dirty, is always honest and great at rodeos.

PINKIE PIE

She's giggly, playful, super girly and a tremendous ball of energy! Pinkie Pie loves to laugh, loves to talk, and loves to eat sweets! She puts a smile on everyone's face!

FLUTTERSHY

With her trusting nature and gentle ways, Fluttershy is a friend to all the forest animals. She's rather shy, very generous and has an inner strength that appears when trouble arises.

RAINBOW DASH

Capable and athletic, Rainbow Dash lives for adventure. She's brilliant at flying, the first to volunteer for dangerous tasks and is a true action hero!

RARITY

She's possibly the most beautiful unicorn you will ever see — and wants every pony to be beautiful, too! She's very creative, an amazing fashion designer and has a heart of gold.

And not forgetting!
SPIKE THE DRAGON

This cute baby dragon helps Twilight with her studies and missions from Princess Celestia.

TWILIGHT'S MAGICAL FUN!

Help her solve these problems!

True or false?

1 Rainbow Dash has blue eyes. T F

2 There are six ponies in the picture. T F

3 Only Rarity and Twilight are unicorns. T F

4 Fluttershy has a yellow mane. T F

5 Pinkie Pie is holding a trumpet. T F

6 Applejack is wearing a scarf. T F

Starry Secret!

Use the code to read
Twilight's secret message

e   i

a   Code   o

u

w ⊙ s r ★★ s o d
⊙ n Pr ⊙ nc ⊙ ss
C ⊙ l ⊙ st ★★ 's
c ⊙★ rt ★ n C ⊙ nt ⊙ rl ⊙ t

Spot Spike

Three pictures of Spike,
but which one is different?

a   b   c

Answers
on page 62!

MAY THE BEST PET WIN!

Fluttershy knows that pets make wonderful friends, but will she find the perfect pet for Rainbow Dash?

1 Rainbow Dash is having a lovely afternoon nap in a tree, when she's woken by a lot of noise.

2 It's Twilight, Applejack, Rarity, Fluttershy and Pinkie Pie playing with their pets in the park. "We were going to invite you," says Pinkie Pie. "But then Twilight remembered that you don't even have a pet!"

3 Fluttershy shows her lots of different animals, certain that one would make the perfect pet for Rainbow Dash. "How about a cutesy, wootsy bunny, or a widdle puddy tat?" asks Fluttershy. But Rainbow Dash only wants a pet that can fly as fast as she can.

"Or a ladybug?"

"Or a cute cricket?"

4 "What about a seal?" cries Fluttershy.

5 None of these are good enough. "It has to be awesome, flying and cool!" Rainbow Dash says. So Fluttershy gets together all of the coolest, most awesome flying creatures she can find, and Rainbow decides to have a competition to see which one is best.

6 The creatures line up. "This competition isn't for the weak!" cries Rainbow Dash. "Any questions?"

7 "I've got a question," whispers Applejack. "Does she understand what a pet needs?" "Yeah," agrees Twilight. "Like care, love and affection..."

8 Just then Rainbow Dash sees a tortoise in the line up. She's not happy! "He's always dreamed of being somepony's pet," explains Fluttershy. "Just let him try."

9 The first round in the competition is speed. The falcon whizzes across the finish line first while the tortoise hasn't even crossed the starting line!

10 Now it's the agility round, and the animals make their way through hoops, turnstiles and other obstacles. The hummingbird easily wins this, while the poor tortoise can't get off the ground.

11 The tortoise performs the worst in every round. He's not stylish, isn't awesome and isn't radical enough for Rainbow Dash.

12 For the guts round, the creatures have to try to get Opal's favourite toy away from her. The buttefly manages this with ease!

13 The final round is a race against Rainbow Dash herself!

15 "Easy peasy!" cries Rainbow as she races ahead, but she's not looking where she's going. SMACK! She flies straight into the side of a ravine and causes an avalanche.

14 The remaining creatures in the competition fly along treacherous routes following Rainbow, while the tortoise slowly trudges along.

16 As Rainbow dodges the falling rocks, the eagle, falcon, owl and bat overtake her. Rainbow is knocked to the ground and her wing gets stuck under a falling rock. "Come back!" she cries. But they're too far away to hear her.

17 Then Rainbow hears something coming, it's the tortoise. "You!" she cries. "The most annoying turtle in the world!"

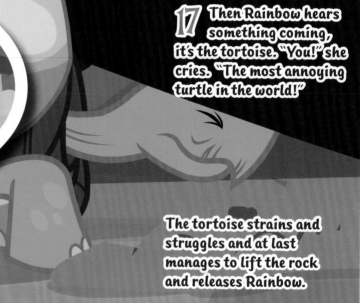

The tortoise strains and struggles and at last manages to lift the rock and releases Rainbow.

19 While the eagle came first in the race, Rainbow says the winner was the one who crossed the line with her — and that was the tortoise who helped her when she needed it.

18 Meanwhile, the ponies are waiting to see who will win. Eventually Rainbow appears, on the back of the tortoise!

20 Later, Rainbow flies off for her first pony-pet playdate. With Tank the tortoise, her new pet, flying after her in his customised flying shell!

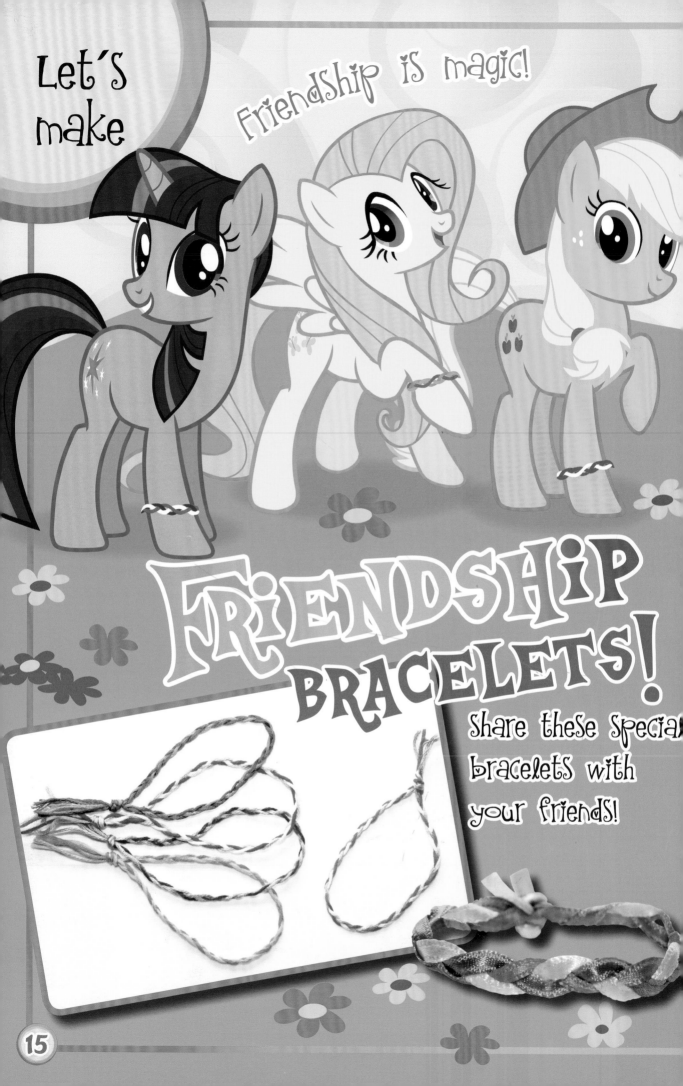

Let's make

Friendship is magic!

FRiENDSHiP BRACELETS!

Share these special bracelets with your friends!

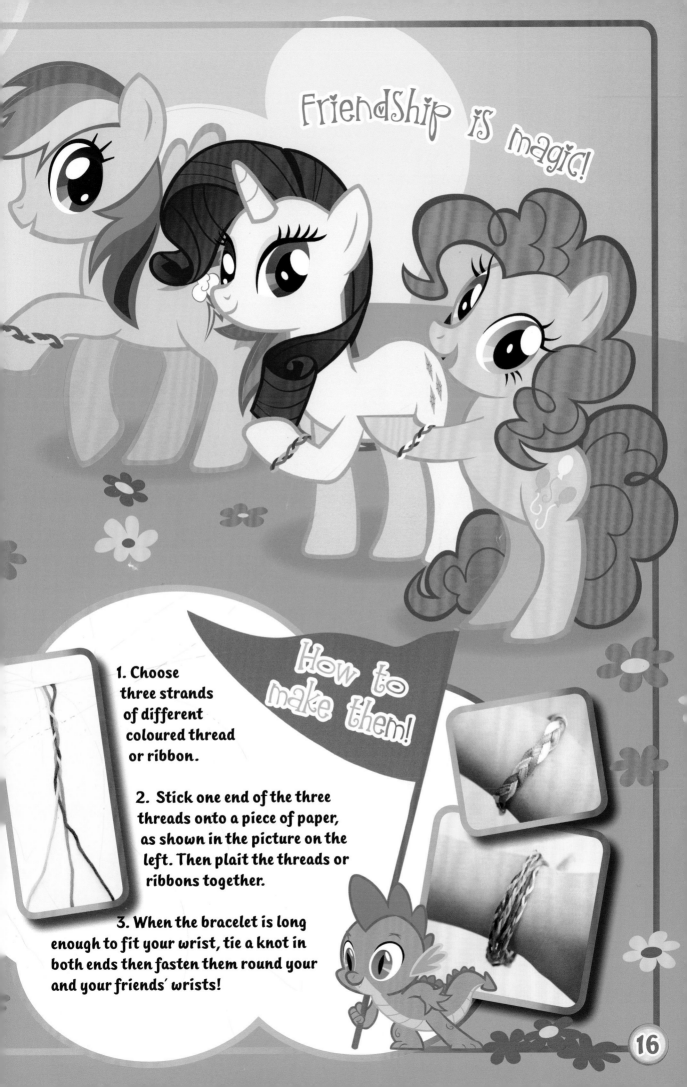

Friendship is magic!

How to make them!

1. Choose three strands of different coloured thread or ribbon.

2. Stick one end of the three threads onto a piece of paper, as shown in the picture on the left. Then plait the threads or ribbons together.

3. When the bracelet is long enough to fit your wrist, tie a knot in both ends then fasten them round your and your friends' wrists!

WHAT CAN YOU SPOT?

Can you spot all these little pictures in the big picture of SugarCube Corner, Pinkie Pie's favourite shop!

17

Tick them off when you find them all!

WHICH PONY

Find out with our quiz

Mostly a
You're like TWILIGHT SPARKLE! She loves to learn and read books, too.

Mostly b
Just like RAINBOW DASH you're very sporty and like to do exciting things.

HE, HE!

HA, HA!

Mostly c
You're as funny as PINKIE PIE and are always giggling with your friends.

1 It's your birthday! How would you like to celebrate with your friends?

a A stargazing sleepover

b A day at an exciting theme park

c See a funny film and eat popcorn

d A pampering beauty session

e Visit a wildlife sanctuary

f Cook scrummy things

3 What do you love to do at school?

a Read

b PE

c Playtime

d Art

e Singing

f Gardening

19

ARE YOU?

Tick your answers!

2 Which pet would you most like?

- A A cute chameleon ◯
- B A dog to run around with ◯
- C A talking parrot ◯
- D A pretty kitten ◯
- E A cuddly rabbit ◯
- F A pony to ride ◯

Mostly d
Just like RARITY, you're very creative and adore fashion and giving your friends makeovers.

Mostly e
You love to sing, are a friend to all the animals and are as gentle and caring as FLUTTERSHY.

4 What would you like to be when you're grown-up?

- A A teacher ◯
- B An Olympic athlete ◯
- C A sweetshop owner ◯
- D A fashion designer ◯
- E A vet ◯
- F A gardener ◯

Mostly f
You're very practical, not afraid of getting dirty and very honest, just like APPLEJACK!

PRINCESS CELESTIA PAIRS!

Draw a line to the pairs of Princess Celestia which are the same. Circle round the picture which doesn't have a pair!

Answer on page 62

Part 1

A Canterlot Wedding!

What exciting news! There's going to be a wedding in Canterlot and all of the ponies have been asked to help with the preparations...

1 Spike gives Twilight a special scroll from Princess Celestia. "I will be presiding over the wedding ceremony," reads Twilight to her friends. "But would very much like you and your friends to help with the preparations for this wonderful ceremony." Fluttershy and her songbird choir are asked to provide the music. Rarity is asked to design dresses for the bride and bridesmaids.

2 Applejack will be in charge of the catering for the reception which Pinkie Pie will host. Rainbow Dash is asked to perform a Sonic Rainboom for the bride and groom. While Twilight has been given the most important job of all — making sure everything goes as planned.

Pinkie Pie does three backflips in delight!

Rarity is so thrilled to be asked to design the dresses that she faints!

3 "But who's getting married?" Spike coughs up another letter from Princess Celestia. It says the bride is Princess Mi Amore Cadanza and the groom is Twilight's brother, Shining Armor, the Captain of the Royal Guard — Why didn't he tell her he was getting married?

4 The ponies are so excited as they travel on the Friendship Express train to Canterlot Castle for the wedding.

5 "How dare you not tell me you were getting married?" cries Twilight when she sees her brother Shining Armor.

6 Shining Armor explains that a threat has been made to Canterlot and he has been busy keeping Canterlot safe with an electric force-field.

7 "Will you be my Best Mare?" Shining Armor asks his little sister. Twilight's delighted, especially when she hears that Princess Mi Amore Cadanza is actually Princess Cadance, who used to foalsit Twilight when she was little. She's the most beautiful, kind, caring pony ever!

8 But when Princess Cadance sees Twilight she doesn't remember her at all and isn't happy with any of the wedding plans.

9 When Cadance tries some of Applejack's wedding food, she says she loves it but Twilight sees her putting it in the bin...

10 ...then Princess Cadance rudely tells Rarity she doesn't like any of the dresses she's designed.

11 Twilight tells her pony friends that this Princess Cadance isn't like the lovely pony she knew, but they think she's jealous of her. Especially when Princess Cadance asks them all to be her bridesmaids. But Twilight's sure that Princess Cadance has put a spell on her brother.

12 Later on, Princess Celestia oversees the wedding rehearsal. Everyone is there — the pony bridesmaids, Spike, Princess Cadance, Shining Armor and his Groomcolts. Everyone that is, apart from Twilight Sparkle.

13 Twilight Sparkle suddenly appears. "You have to listen to me! She's evil!" she cries pointing at Princess Cadance. But still, nobody will believe what she says and Princess Cadance runs off in tears.

14 "You can forget about being my Best Mare," shouts Shining Armor to his sister. "In fact, if I were you, I wouldn't show up to the wedding at all!" Everyone is shocked by Twilight's behaviour!

16 Twilight awakes in darkness, in the crystal caves beneath Canterlot with Princess Cadance. The REAL Princess Cadance. "The Cadance that brought you down here was an imposter. I've been imprisoned like you!" she says and sings a song which Twilight recognises, it's a song they sang together when Twilight was young.

15 The ponies all go, leaving Twilight distraught. But Princess Cadance returns. She fires up her horn and POOF! Twilight disappears into thin air!

27

Turn to page 37 to finish the story!

SPOT THE DIFFERENCES

Can you spot the 10 differences between these two pictures of Princess Cadance?

Answers on page 62!

Tick a heart every time you spot one!

28

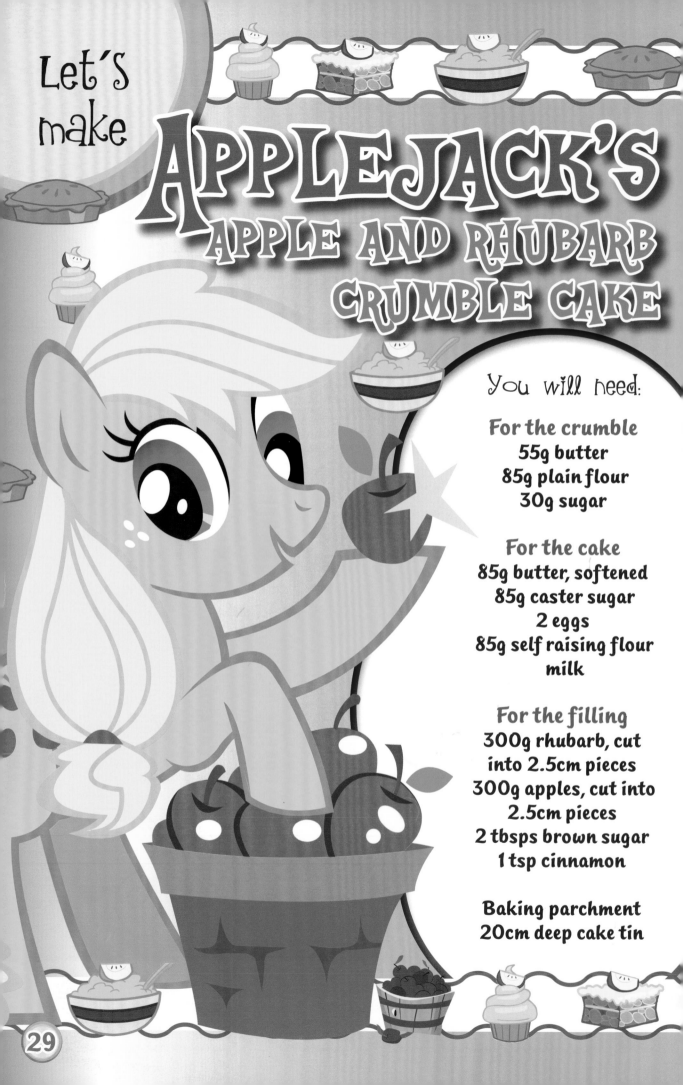

Let's make

APPLEJACK'S
APPLE AND RHUBARB CRUMBLE CAKE

You will need:

For the crumble
55g butter
85g plain flour
30g sugar

For the cake
85g butter, softened
85g caster sugar
2 eggs
85g self raising flour
milk

For the filling
300g rhubarb, cut into 2.5cm pieces
300g apples, cut into 2.5cm pieces
2 tbsps brown sugar
1 tsp cinnamon

Baking parchment
20cm deep cake tin

Always ask an adult to help when cooking!

What to do:

1. Ask an adult to heat the oven to 180°C/gas mark 4. Line the cake tin with baking parchment.
2. Make the crumble topping by rubbing the butter into the flour with your fingers, then stir in the sugar. Put to one side.
3. Make the cake by mixing the butter and sugar until pale and light and fluffy. Gradually beat in the eggs, then mix in the flour. Add a little milk if your mixture is too stiff.
4. Pour the cake mixture into your prepared tin and smooth it over. Place the fruit in an even layer on top, then scatter the sugar and cinnamon all over. Then sprinkle the crumble

mixture on the top.
5. Ask an adult to put it in the oven and bake for 45-55 minutes. The top should be firm and the crumble mix golden. Allow to cool in the tin and then carefully lift out.
6. It's ready to serve!

Apple Search

Can you find these other apple treats hiding on the page?

6 apple pies

5 bowls of apple porridge

4 apple cupcakes

3 apple loaves

2 buckets of apples

Rarity's
Fashion and Beauty Tips

She's the most beautiful unicorn in Ponyville!

She's a beauty!

When Rarity prances down the street, every pony can't help but stare at her! Her purple mane is always glossy and shiny, her white coat gleams and her bright eyes dazzle. She loves to have pampering bubbly baths, makes sure her mane is clean and conditioned and always smells sweet!

Healthy food!

One of Rarity's biggest beauty tips is to eat as healthily as possible. That means eating lots of delicious fresh fruit and crunchy vegetables every day, and keeping sweets and chocolate just for special occasions.

Salon Style!

Rarity loves experimenting with different hairstyles. Sometimes she'll have her mane straight, sometimes curly and on very special occasions she pins it up high on her head. Whatever style she has, she always has a comb with her to keep it neat and tidy.

Accessories!

Rarity knows that you don't have to spend a lot of money to look fabulous. Pretty hairbands and ribbons, sparkly jewellery and special scarves are all you need to make you look super-stylish and stand out from the crowd.

Fashion queen!

Rarity's an amazing fashion designer and her spectacular creations are admired by everyone. Her biggest dream is to one day design an outfit for Princess Celestia herself, but in the meantime her wonderful designs can be bought at Ponyville's Carousel Boutique!

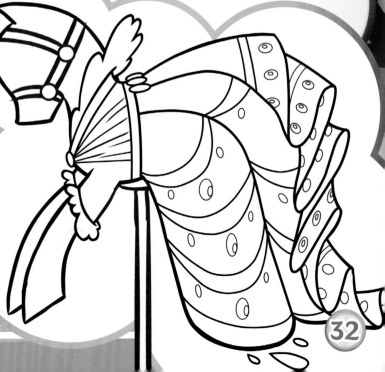

TOP TIP! Rarity loves pretty colours – make this gown look really beautiful!

MEET FLUTTERSHY'S

Spot the difference

There are six differences between these pictures. Tick a box everytime you spot one.

Feathered friends

How many of Fluttershy's bird friends can you count on the page, including this one and the ones on the spot the difference pictures? Write the number here.

17

Answers on page 62

FRIENDS!

Fluttershy quiz!

How much do you know about her?

1. Where does Fluttershy live?
a. in a castle ☐
b. in a treehouse ☐
c. in a cottage ☑

2. Fluttershy is very good at...
a. dancing ☐
b. singing ☑
c. playing the piano ☐

3. Fluttershy is very...
a. noisy ☐
b. grumpy ☐
c. shy ☑

4. Her cutie mark is...
a. butterflies ☑
b. rabbits ☐
c. birds ☐

ANGEL PAIRS

Angel is Fluttershy's pet rabbit. Match the pairs of Angels that are the same, then find the one that doesn't have a pair.

A Canterlot Wedding! Part 2

Continued from page 27

1 Meanwhile the imposter Princess Cadance is preparing for her wedding. She's actually the evil Queen Chrysalis and she's feeding off Shining Armor's love, making him weaker and weaker so she can take over Equestria.

2 Twilight and the real Princess Cadance escape from the crystal caves and rush to the wedding, just as Princess Celestia is about to perform the ceremony.

3 Everyone's shocked to see two Princess Cadances. "She's a changeling," explains the real Princess Cadance.

4 There's a sudden flash of green light and Imposter Cadance changes into evil Queen Chrysalis...

5 ...a gangly black pegacorn! She reveals that Shining Armor is in her control and his protection spell around Equestria is getting weaker and weaker. The wedding party and guests gasp in horror. "Soon my Changeling Army will take Canterlot and then we will take all of Equestria!" she cries.

6 Even Princess Celestia's magical powers aren't strong enough to fight off the evil Queen Chrysalis and she's knocked to the floor.

7 Princess Celestia sends the ponies off to find the Elements of Harmony at the Cathedral of Harmony. Only they can defeat the evil Queen.

8 At the Cathedral of Harmony, the ponies are met by a whole army of Changelings who have broken through Shining Armor's weakened spell.

9 As the ponies prepare to take on the Changelings, the Changelings transform themselves into imposter ponies. The ponies aren't sure who's an imposter or not, but a magic spell helps them defeat the Changelings.

FLASH!

10 The ponies run back to the wedding. While the evil Queen talks, Princess Cadance sneaks over to Shining Armor. She aims her horn and FLASH! a pink spark zaps him and wakes him up. Their love together defeats the evil queen and her Changeling army.

11 Now the evil queen has gone, the proper wedding can take place. The real Princess Cadance loves all the food that Applejack has cooked!

12 She adores Rarity's wedding dress!

13 She loves Fluttershy's beautiful music.

14 And thinks Pinkie Pie's party ideas are wonderful!

40

15 Spike makes a brilliant ring bearer.

16 The couple are married at long last!

17 The whole of Equestria celebrates with Princess Cadance and Shining Armor.

18 And it's all thanks to Twilight!

19 "Let's get this party started!" cries Pinkie Pie as the reception begins!

WEDDING SNAPSHOTS

Wonderful pictures from a wonderful day!

Beautiful bridesmaids!

Applejack provides the music!

Princess Cadance is a radiant bride!

Wow! A Sonic Rainboom from Rainbow Dash!

Spike is such a cool dancer!

Rarity catches the bouquet!

Twilight sings a special song!

Pinkie Pie spins the decks!

Fireworks end the special day!

The newly weds are sooo in love!

Let's make

STRAWBERRY MILKSHAKE

with Pinkie Pie

You will need:
- 250g strawberries
- 1 banana
- 175ml cold milk
- Scoop of vanilla or strawberry ice cream

What to do:
1. Wash, destalk and chop the strawberries.
2. Peel and slice the banana.
3. Put all the fruit, milk and ice cream in a blender and whiz together until smooth.
4. Pour into glasses and they're ready to drink. Yum!

Always ask an adult to help when cooking!

Fabulous fruits!
You can make these with lots of different delicious fruits too! Try raspberries, peaches, blueberries, bananas or your other favourite fruit. Or whiz lots of different fruits together for a super-scrummy shake!

makes 2 to 3 Servings!

Colour in Pinkie Pie

RACE TO SCHOOL

Play this game with your friends!

START 1

2 Give teacher an apple. Move forward 2.

16

17

18 Stop for a snack. go back 2.

19

3

4

Stop to pick flowers. go back 1. 5

Sweetie Belle

Scootaloo

Apple Bloom

You'll need a dice and three counters to play!

How to play:
1 Each player takes a counter and chooses which little pony they want to be.
2. Take turns to throw the dice then follow the instructions on the circle.
3. First one to school wins!

RAINBOW DASH

She is the most exciting pony in Ponyville!

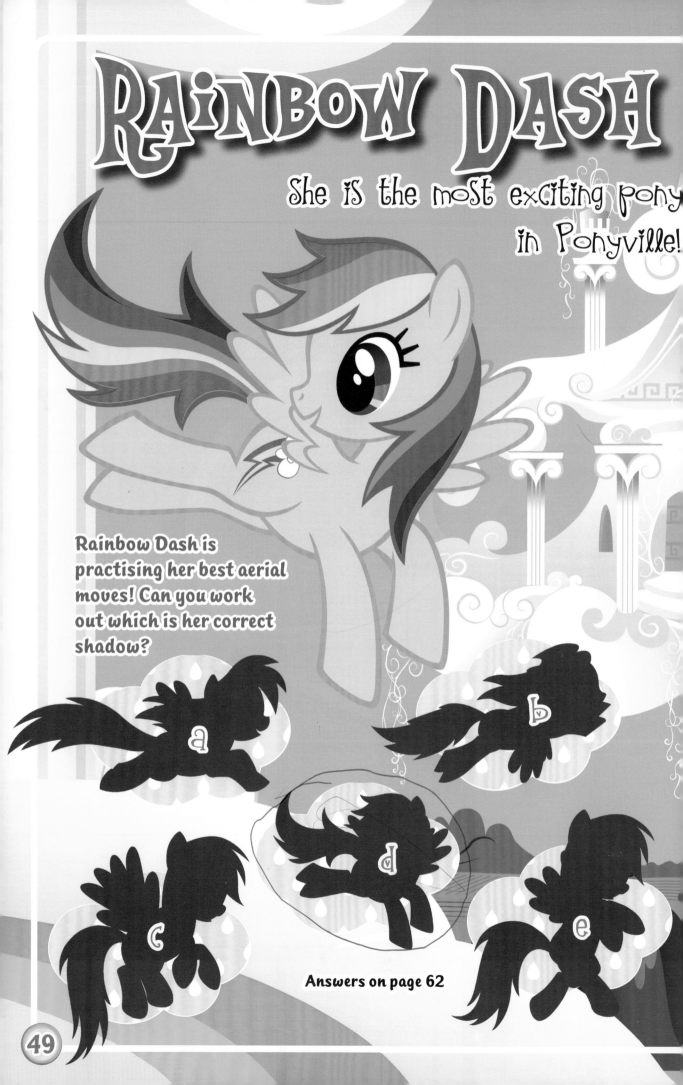

Rainbow Dash is practising her best aerial moves! Can you work out which is her correct shadow?

a

b

c

d

e

Answers on page 62

PUZZLES

Fill in the missing words and when you read the letters down, you'll find Rainbow Dash's favourite hobby.

1. f **a s t**

1. Not slow!

2. **s k i** l l

2. Be able to do something really well!

3. **s k** y

3. It's up above!

4. **f r i e n d**

4. Rainbow Dash is a very good one!

5. **N**

5. The 14th letter of the alphabet!

6. g **r a s s**

6. It's on the ground!

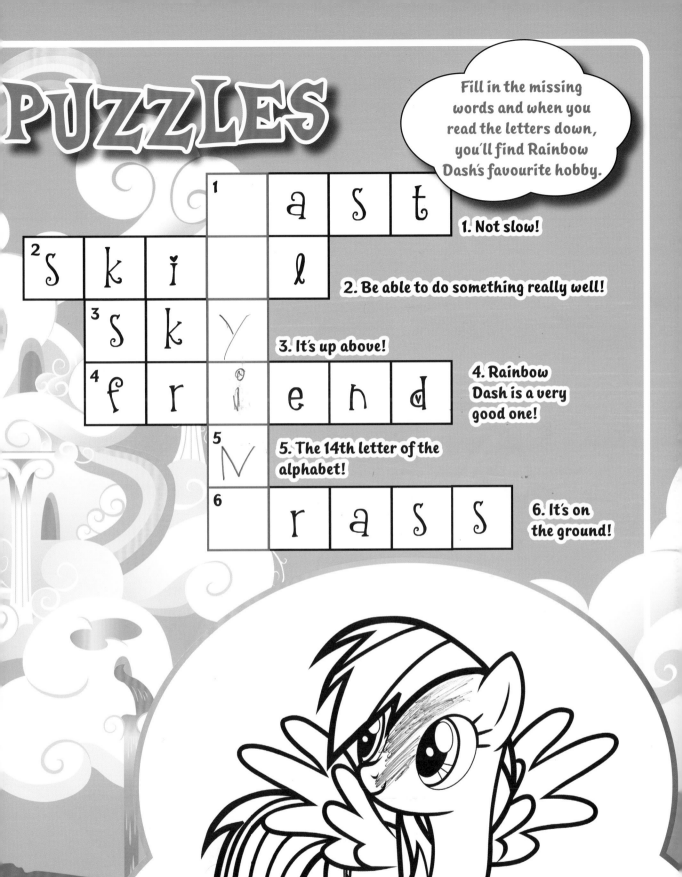

Colour in Rainbow Dash

50

FLUTTERSHY

BUNTING

This will look so pretty on your bedroom wall!

Always ask an adult to help when using scissors!

How to make it

1 Trace over the white butterfly shapes. Then use the traced shapes as templates to cut out butterfly shapes onto thin coloured card.
2 Make small holes in the corners of each of the card butterfly's top wings.
3 Thread ribbon or thread through each hole and tie together with bows.
4 Then stick the thread at each end of the bunting to your wall.

52

SISTERHOOVES SOCIAL

Sweetie Belle's spending the week with her big sister, Rarity, while her parents are on holiday. Sweetie Belle's keen to help Rarity as much as she can, but Rarity's a very fussy sister...

1 ...and everything Sweetie Belle does ends in disaster. She burns the breakfast...

...shrinks Rarity's favourite designer sweater...

...and uses Rarity's precious blue sapphires to create a special picture for Rarity! Everything she does makes Rarity cross.

2 "Oh dear Sweetie Belle, what am I going to do with you?" cries Rarity in despair. "We could paint together, ride bikes, sing a song, pillow fight..." suggests Sweetie Belle. "That's not what I meant!" replies Rarity sternly, "while I'm buying more gems, you can put everything back NEATLY!" And she gallops out of the door.

3 While Rarity is out, Sweetie Belle goes into Rarity's designing room . "No wonder she didn't want me to create a mess," sighs Sweetie Belle, looking around, "she already has a mess!" So Sweetie Belle tidies everything away.

4 But Sweetie Belle's done the wrong thing again! "This wasn't a mess!" cries Rarity when she returns. "It was ORGANIZED chaos. I was finishing my new fashion line and you went and put it all away! I need time alone!" So Sweetie Belle sadly leaves her big sister's house .

SISTERHOOVES SOCIAL

5 As Sweetie Belle mopes in Ponyville Townsquare she bumps into Apple Bloom and she tells her friend all what's happened. "You should do the Sisterhooves Social!" cries Apple Bloom. "Sister teams compete against other sisters. Applejack and I do it every year, and you and Rarity should do it!"

6 Sweetie Belle thinks it's an excellent idea, but Rarity doesn't — it sounds too dirty for her! "Well then. I'll try the Sisterhooves Social without a sister! In fact, I think I'll try the rest of my life without a sister!" cries Sweetie Belle and storms out.

7 At Sweet Apple Acres, Sweetie Belle is telling Applejack and Apple Bloom all what's happened. "Rarity will come round," Applejack reassures her, "sisters always do!"

8 Meanwhile, Rarity is realising she shouldn't have been mean to Sweetie Belle. Thanks to Sweetie Belle's tidying up, Rarity has been inspired to create a fabulous Rainbow Connection Collection...

9 ...the sweater which Sweetie Belle shrank is the perfect fit for Opal the cat...

10 ...and when she finds the picture which Sweetie Belle made for her, using Rarity's special gems, Rarity realises how special her sister Sweetie Belle is. "I will never be sisterless again!" she vows!

11 Rarity tries to make up with Sweetie Belle, but Sweetie Belle would rather have Applejack as a sister "Oh Rarity! Being a sister is give and take," Applejack tells her. Rarity plans how to show Sweetie Belle how much she cares for her.

12 The following day the Sisterhooves Social gets underway. "Applejack and I figured that since we do this every year...I'd let you borrow my sis!" cries Apple Bloom. Sweetie Pie is thrilled to have Applejack as her sister.

13

"On your marks, get set, gooooooo!"

14 And they're off! But at the first obstacle — a muddy pool — Applejack slips. She quickly gets to her feet and the pair race off.

15 They gobble up the cherry pies faster than any other team...

...are really quick at pushing the hay bales...

...are brilliant at getting juice out of grapes...

...and cleverly carry eggs together without breaking any.

16 But after a very close run, they're pipped at the post and come second.

17 "Thank you!" squeals Sweetie Belle. "I don't care that we didn't win! This was SO much fun." But as she leaps up to hug her, she knocks Applejack's hat off, revealing a horn!

18 It's Rarity who raced with Sweetie Pie, not Applejack! They'd swapped place with each other at the very first mud hole.

19 Back at Rarity's house, Spike is helping Rarity and Sweetie Belle write a letter to Princess Celestia to say what they have learned. "Having a sister is just about the bestest thing in the world, but it isn't easy!" says Sweetie Belle. "I agree," joins in Rarity. "It takes teamwork and compromise but mostly it's about having fun together."

PUZZLE ANSWERS

My Little Pony

Page 7 Twilight's Magical Fun
1 False; 2 True; 3 True; 4 False;
5 False; 6 False
The secret message is: I was raised in
Princess Celestia's Canterlot Court
Spike C is different

Page 33 Fluttershy's Friends
Spot the differences

Fluttershy quiz
1 c; 2 b; 3 c; 4 a
Feathered Friends: 17

This Angel
doesn't have a pair

Page 21 Princess Celestia
This one doesn't have a pair

Page 28 Princess Cadence
Spot The Difference

Page 49
Rainbow Dash Puzzles
Shadow d is correct.
The missing word is: flying